DELETE

FAIRFAX PUBLIC LIBRARY
313 Vanderbilt Street
Fairfax, IA 52228
319-846-2894

RALLY CARS

AMAZING RACING CARS

BY ASHLEY GISH

CREATIVE EDUCATION • CREATIVE PAPERBACKS

Published by Creative Education and Creative Paperbacks
P.O. Box 227, Mankato, Minnesota 56002
Creative Education and Creative Paperbacks are imprints of
The Creative Company
www.thecreativecompany.us

Design by The Design Lab
Production by Joe Kahnke
Art direction by Rita Marshall
Printed in China

Photographs by Alamy (Action Plus Sports Images, D Primrose, Russell Hunter, imageBROKER, Hugh Peterswald/Pacific Press Agency), Dreamstime (Kirill Makarov), Getty Images (Imagno/Hulton Archive, The Denver Post), Shutterstock (Shevel Artur, EvrenKalinbacak, Manamana, Artsiom Petrushenka, Vdant85)

Copyright © 2021 Creative Education, Creative Paperbacks
International copyright reserved in all countries. No part of this book may be reproduced in any form without written permission from the publisher.

Library of Congress Cataloging-in-Publication Data
Names: Gish, Ashley, author.
Title: Rally cars / Ashley Gish.
Series: Amazing racing cars.
Includes bibliographical references and index.
Summary: A fast-paced, high-interest introduction to rally cars, modified race cars known for their teams of drivers and use in multi-stage rally races. Also included is a biographical story about rally driver Michèle Mouton.
Identifiers:
ISBN 978-1-64026-290-4 (hardcover)
ISBN 978-1-62832-822-6 (pbk)
ISBN 978-1-64000-420-7 (eBook)
This title has been submitted for CIP processing under LCCN 2019049511.

CCSS: RI.1.1, 2, 4, 5, 6, 7; RI.2.2, 5, 6, 7, 10; RI.3.1, 5, 7, 8; RF.1.1, 3, 4; RF.2.3, 4

First Edition HC 9 8 7 6 5 4 3 2 1
First Edition PBK 9 8 7 6 5 4 3 2 1

Table of Contents

Rally Car Beginnings	4
Rally Teams	7
Tallying Times	11
Speeding through Stages	12
Rough Driving	15
Brakes and Suspension	16
Amazing Rally Cars	20
Driver Spotlight: Michèle Mouton	22
Read More	24
Websites	24
Index	24

Early rally cars were judged on speed as well as looks and comfort.

Rally cars race on roads that have been closed for the competition. Most rally cars look like normal cars. But they have been **modified** for racing. The 1911 Monte Carlo Rally was the first official rally race. Twenty-three cars raced to Monaco from 11 locations in Europe.

modified changed to improve performance

RALLY CARS

Fans can watch stages from just a few feet away from the track.

During a rally, or race, cars drive one at a time through **stages**. Races can last for days. Drivers try to get the fastest time at each stage. Before the rally begins, fans can walk around the **parc expose**. Teams prepare for the race.

parc expose the area where all the rally cars are parked before a race

stages short, closed sections of road with a starting and finishing point

The co-driver and driver usually talk through headsets because the car makes so much noise.

A rally team includes a driver and a co-driver. The driver operates the car. The co-driver reads **pace notes** to the driver throughout the race. Team members wear **fire suits**.

fire suits suits made from special material that is resistant to catching fire

pace notes information about the road ahead

RALLY CARS

Rally scores are based on the times of each stage. The car with the fastest total time wins the rally. There can be up to 30 stages per rally. These stages may be spread out. Drivers obey traffic laws when driving between stages.

The times from each stage are added together to decide the rally winner.

Rally cars may reach speeds of 100 miles (161 km) per hour. Only one car at a time races in each stage. This helps prevent crashes.

A metal roll cage helps keep team members safe in case of a rollover.

13

RALLY CARS

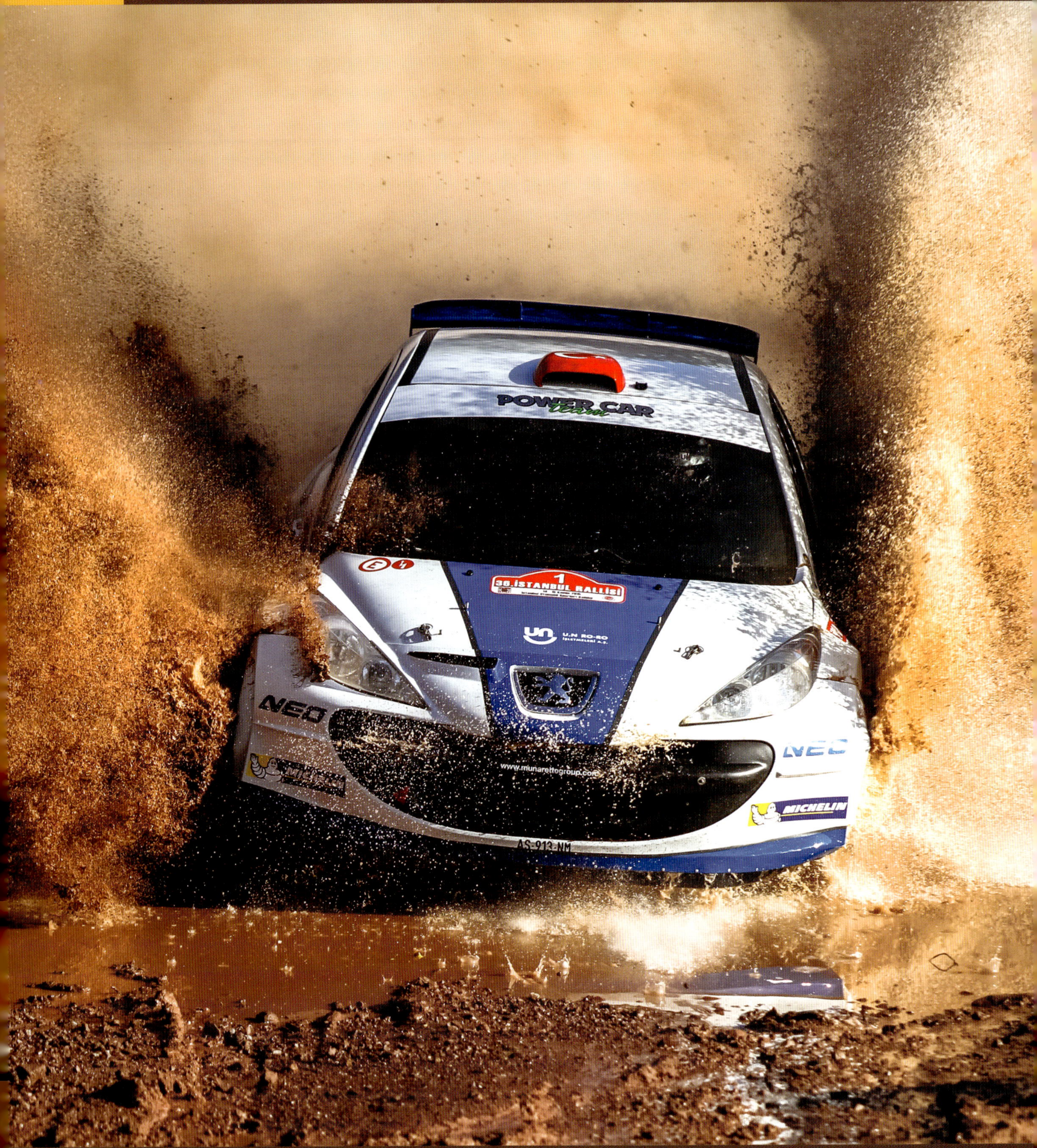
POWER CAR
NEO
NEC
MICHELIN

Rally cars drive on rough roads. A strong skid plate protects the underside of the car. Good tires are important, especially on gravel or snow.

Drivers must be prepared for all types of weather and road conditions.

RALLY CARS

Rally cars are lighter weight and more powerful than normal cars.

Rally cars need good brakes. Sturdy mounts keep cars' **engines** stable during races. A good **suspension** system offers a more comfortable ride over bumpy roads.

engines machines that make vehicles move by burning fuel

suspension the system of springs and shock absorbers that gives a vehicle stability

17

RALLY CARS

Each stage of a race can be up to 30 miles (48.3 km) long.

The World Rally Championship is hosted by the FIA. These races take place across the globe. The American Rally Association hosts the ARA National Championship in the United States.

FIA Fédération Internationale de l'Automobile, or International Automobile Federation

Rally fans line up to watch races. Brightly painted rally cars zoom by. They speed down gravel roads, up hills, and around sharp corners.

Drivers in the World Rally Championship race from January through November.

Driver Spotlight: Michèle Mouton

Michèle

Mouton was born in Grasse, France, in 1951. She became co-driver for a friend in 1972. Her father encouraged her to try driving. She started racing in 1974. Michèle won four World Rally Championship races to place second overall in 1982. She was the first woman to win a World Rally Championship race.

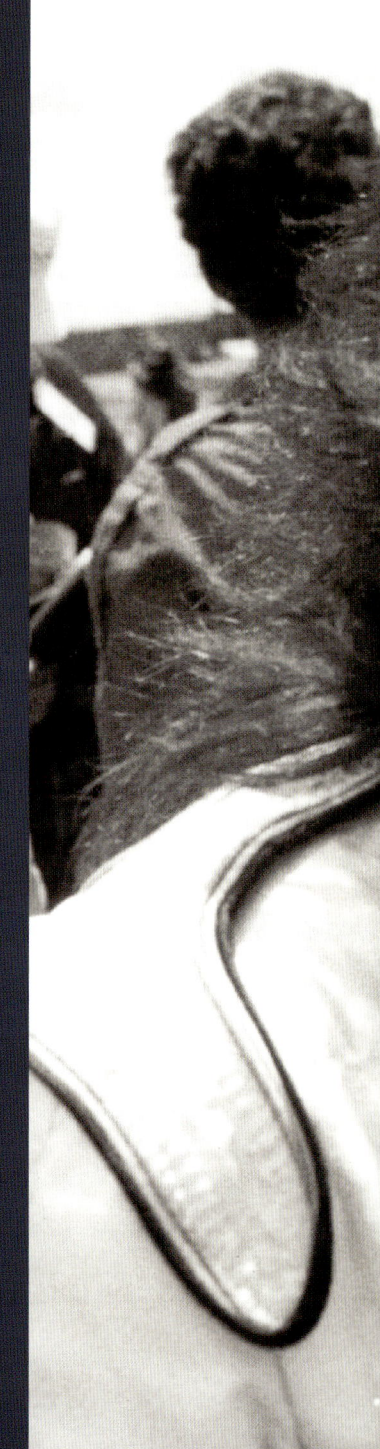

Read More

Bowman, Chris. *Rally Car Racing*. Minneapolis: Bellwether Media, 2016.

Hale, K. A. *Rally Car Racing*. Minnetonka, Minn.: Kaleidoscope, 2019.

Howell, Brian. *Rally Car Racing: Tearing It Up*. Minneapolis: Lerner, 2014.

Websites

DK Find Out: History of Cars
https://www.dkfindout.com/us/transportation/history-cars
Learn more about how cars have developed through time.

Kiddle: Auto Racing Facts for Kids
https://kids.kiddle.co/Auto_racing
Read more about rally cars and other motorsports.

YouTube: Rally Car Racing
https://www.youtube.com/watch?v=1971DmZC41s
Watch a video about rally cars and races.

Note: Every effort has been made to ensure that the websites listed above are suitable for children, that they have educational value, and that they contain no inappropriate material. However, because of the nature of the Internet, it is impossible to guarantee that these sites will remain active indefinitely or that their contents will not be altered.

Index

drivers 7, 8, 11, 22
fans 7, 20
Mouton, Michèle 22
races 4, 7, 8, 11, 19, 22
safety 8, 12

speeds 12
stages 7, 11, 12
suspension 16
teams 7, 8
tires 15